BABY FEVER

A REAL MAN, 3

JENIKA SNOW

BABY FEVER (A Real Man, 3)

By Jenika Snow

www.JenikaSnow.com

Jenika_Snow@Yahoo.com

Copyright © August 2016 by Jenika Snow

First E-book Publication: August 2016

Photographer: Wander Aguiar

Cover model: Jacob Hogue

Photo provided by: Wander Book Club

Cover Designer: Lori Jackson

A REAL MAN SERIES

ALL BOOKS CAN BE READ IN ANY ORDER

Lumberjack

Virgin

Baby Fever

Experienced

Roommate

Arrogant

Feral

Dirty

Viking

Blacksmith

Brutal

Kilt Me

Mine

Alpha Male

Animal

Nailed

Baby Maker

Berserker

He's done being the bad boy ... he's ready to be a father.

Dex

I'm the bad boy— the one mothers warn their daughters about. But I've never seen myself settling down, and that's been fine with me. Then life, reality, whatever you want to call it, bitch slapped me right across the face, and I knew what I wanted.

A baby.

At thirty-nine, I am having a severe case of baby fever, and that means convincing the one woman I've always wanted but knew was too good for me to be mine and be the mother of my child.

Eva

I've always wanted Dex. It's hard not to want a man like Dex. He's all raw power and cut muscle. He's the epitome of what a real man is, but he's not a bastard about it.

But then he throws me a curve ball and says he wants me not only as his woman ... but as the mother of his child.

And I'll be honest; it's what I've always wanted.

Dex

The truth is Eva deserves better than me, but I'm too self-ish, and I want her too badly to back away.

Nothing will stop me from making her mine ... and putting my baby inside her.

Warning: This book is short and right to the point—like the kind of story that gives you whiplash. If you enjoy unbelievable plots, and insta-everything going on, you may enjoy this dirty little read.

1

Dex

I had a severe case of baby fever going on, and I knew exactly which woman I wanted to help me get what I needed.

Eva.

Fucking Eva with her lush curves and hips that are wide and meant to carry my child. I could come just looking at her.

All I could think about was breeding with her, filling her with my spunk, and making her mine.

And she would be mine.

I nearly groaned at the thought of having her, of her being mine.

I'd known her for years, but she was too good for me, too sweet.

But I was also too fucking selfish to let her get away.

I had a reputation for getting into trouble and starting fights with assholes that looked at me the wrong way.

What I didn't have a reputation for was being a womanizer. I was picky as fuck with the females I let into my bed. But they were also empty fucks, a night of release because I was wound up.

What I wanted with Eva was more than just a few hours between the sheets, but I didn't even know if she'd give me the time of day.

She never had before, and a part of me wanted her even more because of it. My bad boy reputation didn't make her a clinger, and she sure as fuck didn't present herself to me like an animal in heat.

Yeah, she would be mine.

I reached down and adjusted my cock. It was rock hard and pressed against the zipper of my jeans.

I focused on Eva again, watching her get the drink order from the bar, and then she made her way toward the table. The bar I was in, and the one she worked at, was the only decent hangout place in this town. But I didn't give a shit about hanging out or getting drunk. I came here to see her.

I finished off the last of my beer, set the bottle aside, and didn't care if I was being obvious in checking out Eva.

"Another one?" Jarren, the owner of the bar and a good friend, asked as he took the empty beer bottle off the table.

"Nah, I'm good," I said, my focus still on Eva. "Wait," I ended up saying to Jarren. "Yeah, I'll take another." It would give me an excuse to loiter here and check out Eva. I also needed to figure out how in the hell I was going to make her mine.

If Eva knew what I was thinking right now, how I wanted to lift up that skirt of hers, pull her panties aside, and plunge my dick in her, she'd probably think I was a sick fuck. But hell, I wanted to do more than that. I wanted to go raw inside her, fill her with my cum, and put my baby in her belly.

I wanted to breed with her like I was some kind of fucking animal. I wanted her to grow big with my child, and just thinking about getting her pregnant made me hard.

I was so damn hard.

I was ready to settle down with the one woman I'd never gone after for fear of shit getting weird between her brother and me. But fuck that. I was older and knew what I wanted. I wanted Eva as mine.

Only mine.

———

Eva

I COULD FEEL his eyes on me. It was like fingers skating

down my spine. To say I was affected was an under-statement.

I wanted Dex. I always have.

To say I didn't get wet because of his bad boy attitude, his hard demeanor, or the fact I knew he liked to skate with trouble back in the day, would have been a bold faced lie.

He'd been a friend of my brother, Charlie, for years. I didn't think Charlie would give a shit if I had something going on with his friend, but Dex has never really seen me as anything more than Charlie's little sister. At least, I never felt like he did.

Although for a while now, I'd seen the way he watched me: with this intensity in his eyes that set me on edge and made me question my good intentions.

What good intentions? You've wanted Dex to fuck you for so long you can't even be next to him without getting wet.

"Hey, you with us or what, Sugar?" Jarren asked.

I glanced at my boss, trying to clear my head. "I'm fine," I said and cleared my throat.

"Well, you want to take this beer over to Dex?"

I licked my lips and nodded. The hairs on the back of my neck stood on end, and I glanced over my shoulder to see the man I'd been fantasizing about for far too long staring right at me. He sat in one of the corner tables, the shadows partially concealing him.

A tingle worked its way up my spine.

I grabbed the beer bottle, as well as a few mixed drinks I had to drop off at another table. It would have been smarter for me to give Dex his beer first, that way I had an excuse to leave, but I dropped off the mixed drinks first and made my way over to Dex.

He leaned back, one leg kicked out, his arm thrown over the back of his chair. He had his other arm on the table, his tattooed flesh instantly arousing me.

Who are you kidding? You're perpetually aroused around him.

Taking a steadying breath, I smiled and handed him the beer. But before I could turn and leave, he reached out and took hold of my wrist. I looked down, my throat tight, my heart racing. Even his hands were tattooed, a fact I found so damn hot.

"What's up?" I managed to say, but my voice sounded strained. Some classic rock song was playing from the old as hell jukebox in the corner, and I could make out through my peripheral vision a couple nearly dry humping on the dance floor. But my eyes were trained on Dex, because hell if I could look away.

"What time do you get off?" he asked, and for a second, my heart stopped. I lowered my brows.

"Ten, why?" I managed to tug my arm free, not because I wanted him to stop touching me, but because I was worried he'd feel my hand shaking. I clenched my fingers inward, my nails digging into my palm.

He shrugged his broad shoulders and leaned forward, placing his forearms on the scarred round table. "We haven't caught up, Eva."

A shiver worked its way up my spine at the sound of my name on his lips.

"What's there to catch up with, Dex?" I was starting to sweat.

Truth was this was probably the most interest he'd taken in me in … forever. Sure, he was nice to me, but it was as if he saw me as nothing more than Charlie's little sister. He didn't see me as a friend he wanted to hang out with, and certainly not someone he'd take to his bed.

"Plenty," he said and lifted the corner of his mouth. "How about we hang out after work? Catch-up and all that shit, Eva girl?"

God, he was so handsome. The tattoos were just the icing on the manly cake that made up Dex. I also knew he had both nipples pierced, and I'd heard him talking to Charlie back in the day about getting his dick pierced. Whether the latter was true or not was not something I would probably ever find out.

And then there was his hair, slightly longer and hanging down to his chin when he didn't put it up in a manbun.

You want to stand here and appraise him? God, you probably look like a weirdo not responding.

I swallowed again as memories played through my head.

"Catch up?" I asked.

He nodded and gave me a sexy full-blown grin.

"Maybe the three of us could all hang out? I know Charlie said it's been a while since you guys saw each other." I don't know why I was trying to get my brother in on this, because I did want to hang out with Dex. And being alone with him didn't sound too bad either.

He leaned back again and shook his head, but didn't respond right away. Instead, I saw him looking me up and down. I could have played it off like nothing, but that was not an innocent look.

No, he was eye fucking me.

"I don't think Charlie needs to hang with us. I mean, I have seen him plenty of times. You and I need to rekindle shit, Eva. A little alone time sounds good, right?"

I found myself nodding.

And then I was thinking about the past again.

When he used to come over to hang out with Charlie, they would stay in the garage, working on Charlie's car, drinking beer when our dad wasn't watching, and talking about "pussy." Ten years older than me, I was the stereotypical annoying sister, but as the years passed, my attraction for Dex grew.

It was that age-old trope about the younger woman wanting her older brother's friend.

Yet, I never got the guy.

Now I was hitting twenty-nine, wasn't married, and had no kids; I was in a damn rut.

The truth was there were plenty of times I'd gone for runs in town, or just gone shopping and I'd see families, mothers with their children, newborns crying, babies giggling, and ache to have that in my life.

I was twenty-nine years old, for God's sake, and not getting any younger. My biological clock was ticking, and I wanted to be a mother.

But I didn't want to get knocked up just for the sake of being a mother, and certainly not by some guy I'd just met.

"You want to hang with me, Eva, spend some time together?" His voice was low, coaxing even. "How about I hear you say it?" The rough timbre had this shiver skating up my spine.

No, there was one person I'd always wanted—secretly loved, too—but I knew being anything with Dex was never going to happen.

I knew damn well I was never going to be his. I would never have gorgeous babies with him ... and damn, would his babies be beautiful.

I tried to clear my thoughts, but yeah, it was no use, especially not when he was right in front of me.

I thought about how Dex acted all interested in me. As much as I wanted to play it cool and act like it didn't affect me ... it sure as hell did.

"Yes, I want to spend some time with you." There, I said it. It felt good to admit it, actually.

"Good. That's real good, Eva." He grinned again. "I'll be waiting for you outside when you get off."

I felt my cheeks heat as I thought of all kinds of dirty things when he said "Get off."

For some reason, this felt like I was playing with fire, but hell, I didn't mind getting burned.

2

Dex

I'd just gone all in here, and I didn't know how in the fuck I was going to get Eva to agree to be mine and have my baby. I wanted her like a fiend, and I sure as hell knew she wanted me. She kept zoning in and out there when we were talking, and I wondered if she was thinking dirty shit about me ... like I was of her.

I leaned back against my sixty-nine Mustang, my arms crossed over my chest, and my focus on the two drunken assholes standing by the front entrance. They were loud and obnoxious as fuck, and hearing the lewd comments they were tossing out at the women who were leaving was starting to piss me off.

I might have a reputation in town as being a bad boy,

and gotten into plenty of trouble when I was younger, but I sure as fuck didn't disrespect women.

And then there she was, her focus on her purse as she rummaged through it. I was about to push off the car and walk toward her, but I froze, every muscle in my body tightening when one of the drunken fuckers approached her.

"Hey, baby. You served me drinks tonight, remember?"

"Unfortunately, I do." She didn't even look up as she responded.

I had to smile. My girl was hard as nails and didn't take any shit when the time called for it.

"Hey, you're acting like a little bi—"

She lifted her head then, and the guy stopped speaking. If her stare could kill a man, he would have been in the ground already. "Watch it, asshole."

I could have let her handle it, but the truth was I wanted to be the man that stepped in and took care of his woman.

And she will be my woman.

But, even if I *didn't* want her as mine, I wouldn't have let any bastard speak to a woman like that. I moved toward the pricks, and just when the asshole opened his mouth again, I pulled Eva back behind me. She made this small sound, maybe from shock, or maybe in protest. I didn't care at the moment, though. I was in fight mode;

whether it actually came down to that or not remained to be seen.

"What were you about to say to my woman?" I said through clenched teeth. The fuckers reeked of alcohol, and as they cocked their heads back to look into my face, I couldn't help but feel that predatory sense rise up in me.

They wouldn't push this. They might be drunk, might even be fuckers, but they were in flight mode. I could see it in their eyes. It was that fear, that realization they'd get their asses kicked to next week if they pushed this.

"Whatever," the asshole muttered, and he let his friend take him away. I watched them until they disappeared down the street and then finally turned around and looked at Eva. I couldn't help but grin at the death stare she was giving me.

"I had it under control," she said, and I nodded.

"I know, but I couldn't let a prick shit on you like that. It wouldn't be very gentlemanly of me." I saw the fight drain out of her, and she loosened up a bit.

"Thanks."

I nodded again, feeling pretty fucking proud at her words. Hearing her say that one word made me feel like a real man. I might have only stood up for her, but I would have laid it down to the pavement if it came down to that.

She stared at me for a second, and I saw her start to get nervous. It was a shift in the way she stood, a flutter of her eyes, and the fact she was picking at the strap of her purse, not really realizing it.

"Okay, well, I'll see you around?" She made it sound like a question, even though she knew damn well I wanted to talk with her.

I reached out and grabbed her wrist. God, that spark of electricity was instant and traveled right up my arms. She looked over at me, and our eyes locked.

"I want to talk with you, catch up." I still held her wrist in a loose but solid hold. "Come for a ride with me?" I asked it as a question, but I wouldn't take no for an answer. I wanted her too badly, and I'd made up my mind about what I wanted; I wasn't backing off.

"And where exactly do you want to go?" She lifted an eyebrow, her emotions clear on her face.

I couldn't help but grin, thinking I'd like her in my bed, under me, and filled with my cum. Of course, I wasn't about to go there ... yet. "Anywhere. You can pick. I just want to talk, see how things have been with you."

She looked a bit hesitant, and although I still held her wrist gently in my grasp, I wanted to pull her closer so she slammed into me, so I could feel the womanly curves that made up her body.

"It's late."

"It is." I thought she was going to turn me down, which I'd have to retaliate by insisting we hang out. I'd wanted this for a while, but I guess I just needed some kind of internal kick in the ass to get things going. "But you did admit you wanted to hang out." I grinned.

I was glad I was finally facing my reality and not being a douche and trying to ignore it.

She laughed softly. "Okay, Dex."

I felt her pulse beating rapidly beneath my thumb, and I started stroking her flesh, feeling it increase in speed with each passing caress.

She was so fucking into this, even if she tried to act all nonchalant and shit.

"But how about you follow me? It'll be easier that way. We can go to the lake."

Charlie and I used to go to the lake to get drunk and smoke a little pot way back in the day. Once Eva was sixteen, she'd tagged along with us a few times, sneaking some sips of beer from Charlie's bottle.

Oh yeah, seclusion, a little quiet.

That's exactly what I was fucking talking about.

"Sounds good," I said, acting cool, like I wasn't really fucking looking forward to this. Hell, I wasn't about to fuck Eva tonight, even if my dick got hard just looking at her. But having some alone time with her, working up to getting to where I wanted with her, was a good start.

I finally let go of her wrist and dragged my thumb along her pulse point.

"Lead the way." I grinned. Yeah, this was really fucking good.

3

Eva

I sat on the hood of Dex's Mustang, looking over at the lake and wondering what was really going on. I'd seen Dex around town, and although we'd drifted apart as the years passed, we'd always remained friends. Not like how he was with Charlie, but that was a given since the two of them spent nearly every day together.

I turned and looked at him.

"What's this really about?" I asked, wanting the truth. Did he need something? Was he in trouble? Was this something that Charlie couldn't know about?

A million different things were slamming through my head.

Oh God. What if this has to do with Dex fucking someone

Charlie had been with?

I didn't know how that really worked, but I assumed it would still be fucked up in guy code.

I shook my head, not sure what I'd say or do if that was the case. Hell, that's probably why he was acting all interested in me ... he needed my help.

And maybe I'm just reaching here? Maybe this has nothing more to do than him wanting to hang out with me?

I stared at the lake, the silence stretching. However, it wasn't an uncomfortable one.

"This really is about me wanting to talk."

I looked at him after he spoke. He was watching me intently, the shadows playing across his face. He looked dangerous, in a way, but I liked that.

"That's the truth, Eva."

I heard the sincerity in his voice. Everything in me was on high alert, and just being beside Dex, smelling the heady, masculine scent of his cologne filled my head, made me dizzy.

I was also a little ashamed to admit I was aroused. It had always been like this, though. He'd just walk by and I'd smell him, see the muscles rippling under his clothes, and I'd instantly want him.

"Okay, so what should be talk about?" I tried to sound like this was normal, and although we'd had plenty of talks over the years, this felt different.

This felt intimate.

"How have you been?" he asked, his focus still on me.

I shrugged. "Fine, I guess, if working at the bar and having to beat off the drunks is an accomplishment." I was teasing, but I saw the dark look crossing over his face with each passing second.

"You shouldn't work there," he said, his voice hard.

I smiled, hoping to lighten things. "I was just kidding."

He didn't look convinced.

"Besides, I can handle myself; you know that."

He looked at the lake and I saw his clenched jaw. "Yeah, I know that, but if motherfuckers are bothering you—"

I placed my hand on his forearm, his skin warm, his muscles tense. "Hey," I said softly and waited for him to look at me. "I can handle myself. And if they get out of hand, you know Jarren won't stand for that."

He stared into my eyes for long seconds, not speaking, but even just having his gaze on me I felt like he was stroking his fingers along my bare flesh.

"Yeah, I know, but I still don't like it." He looked down at my hand on his arm, and I was embarrassed I was still touching him. But before I could move it away, he placed his much bigger had over mine. "No, keep it there. I like the way it feels."

God, my heart jumped right into my throat.

I probably should have removed my hand anyway, but I liked the feel of his muscles tensing beneath my palm. I'd caused that, and I could see that reality written on his face. I felt it in the way he tightened his hand on mine.

"You know I always noticed you, Eva."

The way he said those words had my heart stopping a little bit. I knew what *I* wanted him to mean, but that didn't mean that's what this was about.

"I noticed you, too," I said, smiling, but knowing it didn't really reach my eyes.

He didn't speak for long seconds, and as the air between us became heated, thick, I had a very real feeling Dex meant something more ... intimate.

He slowly shook his head, and my throat tightened further.

"Do you understand what I mean?" His voice sounded thick, serious.

I didn't answer, because I didn't know if I wanted to admit anything, at least not right now.

"I've *noticed* you ... for years." His voice was low, soft even.

He leaned in just an inch, and I felt the light puffs of his cinnamon breath brush across my lips. A tingling settled over me, and I had this strange feeling Dex might try to kiss me. And when he lowered his gaze to my mouth, something in me shifted.

I wanted his mouth pressed to mine.

I wanted his tongue moving along mine.

I wanted to be in his bed, under him, with that massive cock I knew he had deep inside of me.

God.

But despite wanting this, fear took hold. I didn't know why I was scared as hell, but either way I tensed. Dex must have sensed that from me because he backed off an inch.

"I..."

What in the hell was I supposed to say? Wasn't this what I'd wanted, to have Dex interested in me?

But instead of embracing it, I was afraid of my own feelings.

"I should probably go." I got off the hood of the car, my legs feeling like they were made of pudding, and my mind swirling with this small exchange. Nothing had even happened, yet I was running.

"Eva," Dex called out, his voice deep but firm. I looked at him and watched as he came closer. God, I wanted him to touch me again. I wanted him to look at my mouth as if he was starving to kiss me.

"You're okay?" he asked, genuine worry in his voice.

"I'm fine. It's just late, and I should be getting home."

"I'll follow you, make sure you get home safely."

"You don't have to." I was trying in vain to keep the shakiness from my voice. I was so aroused, so wet, so needy, that it was hard to even think straight right now.

"I know." He took a step closer. "But I'm going to follow you home and make sure you get in okay." There was this hardness in his voice, this "I'm not taking no for an answer" tone.

I nodded, feeling good that he was firm, that he wasn't letting me back down so easy. Call me weak, but I liked that ... loved that.

"Dex—"

"Don't fight me, Eva."

The way he said that had all these thoughts running through my head.

"Don't fight me while I'm deep inside of you and you're begging for more."

"Don't fight me when I have your hands pinned above your head and I'm owning every part of you."

"Don't fight me as I love you, Eva."

"I won't fight you," I whispered, and I watched as his nostrils flared slightly, as if my words had gone deep inside of him ... as if that's just what he wanted to hear.

"Come on. Let's get you home."

I followed him over to my car, where he opened the door for me. When I bent down to climb in, I swear I heard him inhale deeply right by my hair. This shiver worked its way through me. I looked up at him once I was seated in the driver's seat. I saw how tightly he held onto the door, so much that his knuckles were white. I wished I knew what he was thinking.

"I'll be right behind you." He shut the door, and I sat there thinking about what in the hell was going on.

This felt different, and I didn't know if that was a good or a bad thing.

4

Dex

I'd wanted to stay at the lake longer, talk more with her, but I could see I was freaking her the fuck out.

Hell, if she knew what I really wanted with her, to do to her, she'd probably run for the fucking hills.

But that wasn't going to stop me from going through with this and telling her exactly how I felt and what I wanted.

I pulled into her driveway, right behind her car, and cut the engine. Maybe I should have just watched her walk in the house and drive off, but I wanted Eva like a fucking fiend needing a fix, and there was no point in waiting to tell her any of this.

I cut the engine and got out at the same time she did.

She looked genuinely surprised, but I could also see she was a little happy to see I hadn't just driven off.

"I can get in the house okay." She smiled, and fuck, did it do something nice to my chest.

"I know you can, but just driving off would have been a bastard thing to do, yeah?"

She didn't respond, but started looking nervous. I knew she wanted me, and pretty badly, given the way she'd responded to the little touch I'd given her, the words I'd said, and the fact she'd retreated right before I started to kiss her.

Yeah, this was pretty strange for her, no doubt, but it was right, and I just needed to show her that.

I needed to prove that to her.

She turned and started making her way up to the front door. I knew I should have given her room, but I couldn't fucking help myself. She suddenly stopped, turned, and this hard look crossed her face.

"Dex, I don't know what in the hell is going on, or if you're going through some kind of phase—"

"Phase?" I lifted an eyebrow, knowing my amusement was clear.

She nodded, trying to appear so strong.

It turned me on.

"Yeah, like you've run through all the women in town and I'm the last resort." Her voice was shaky. "Or trying to fuck your friend's sister."

I was getting annoyed, not because she was bringing

any of this up, but because she must actually find truth in some of it.

"You think I sleep around?"

She didn't answer, but started biting her lip.

"You think I want to fuck you because it's some kind of notch on my belt? Like it turns me on because you're my fucking best friend's little sister?"

Again, she said nothing. I took a step closer. "I haven't been with a woman in so long it would be embarrassing if I gave a fuck, Eva." I looked down at her mouth again. "I haven't been with a woman because I'm not interested in them. I know what I want, have finally realized what I've been missing out on, and I'm done with that bullshit." I moved a step closer, and I had to give it to her, she didn't back down. "And for the record, I'd never betray Charlie that way. When I'm with you it's for the right reasons, understand?"

She didn't respond.

This low, almost animalistic sound came from the back of my throat, and I didn't even try to mask it. It was a fucking testament to how much I wanted Eva right now.

"I don't want any woman but you." I saw her throat work, and although this was probably coming out of left field for her, I wasn't going to sugarcoat anything. "You want me to leave right now?" I waited a heartbeat for her to respond. Finally, she shook her head slowly.

"Dex." She whispered my name, and it sounded so fucking sweet coming from her lips.

"I want you," I said again.

And not just for right now.

I wanted her for the rest of my life.

I moved closer to her and placed a hand on either side of her head, caging her in, making her lean right up against the side of the house. I inhaled deeply, smelling the sweet yet fresh and crisp scent of her. It made my cock rock hard.

I leaned in so our faces were only an inch apart.

"You're kind of moving in fast, aren't you?" she asked, trying to sound strong. I could tell she was, but I also heard the tremble in her voice.

I knew, without even touching her, she wanted me. "No, I don't think I'm moving fast at all." I pressed a little closer to her, crowding her, making her know I was serious as a heart attack.

"I don't know what's going on here," she whispered, her eyes wide, her pupils dilated. Oh, she wanted me all right, if her increased breathing and erect nipples were anything to go by. Hell, I could see the hard little tips pushing against the material of her tight top.

"You want me to tell you what's going on, Eva?" She licked her lips, and I lowered my gaze to watch the act. My cock jerked hard, pressing against my zipper, wanting the fuck out.

"Dex." She breathed out my name again, and fuck, it sounded good.

I stared right in her eyes and moved one of my hands

closer to her face so I could run my thumb along the curve of her jaw. I felt her shake slightly, and I leaned loser, my lips nearly brushing her ear. "You've been mine for a long fucking time, Eva." I heard her sharp intake of breath. "But I stayed away because that was the right thing to do." I pulled back so I could look into her eyes again. "It was a stupid move; I can admit that." The moment of silence stretched.

"This is insane."

Yeah, it fucking was, but it was the truth. I wasn't going to hide anything from her.

"You've never shown any interest in me." Her voice was so low, hesitant even.

"We weren't close because you're Charlie's baby sister. That was crossing a fucking line." I heard her swallow.

"I'm still Charlie's little sister." She stated the obvious, and I couldn't help but smirk.

"I realized what I've been missing, Eva. It's the fucking truth. Life bitch slapped me, baby." Her eyebrows pulled down a little. "I'm getting old, and I want to settle down. I want a good woman by my side; I want to have a family I can care and provide for." I continued to stroke my thumb along her jawline. "I won't lie. When I first saw you for the gorgeous woman you are, my first reaction was how badly I wanted to fuck you. I wanted to be inside of you, Eva." I shook my head at my words.

Fuck, I'm a bastard.

She inhaled sharply and parted her lips, as if she couldn't get enough air into her body.

I leaned in another inch until our lips were close enough that when I spoke they'd brush together. "But I haven't been with a woman sexually in years, baby. That's the god's honest truth." I stared into her eyes. "And wanting you, but not having the balls to tell you that has been pretty fucking hard." My heart was beating faster, the adrenaline pumping through my veins. "I've jerked off to you so many times, Eva, just thinking about how fucking gorgeous you are, and how much I want you as mine." She sucked in a breath and I found satisfaction in it. "I can admit to being a motherfucker and being too afraid to make a move on you. I can admit to staying away because I didn't want to rock the boat with you and Charlie." She inhaled slowly, but I could see my words were sinking in. "I can admit that not telling you how I felt was the worst fucking mistake I've ever made."

"Dex," she whispered, her warm, sweet smelling breath moving along my mouth and making my cock jerk even harder. "I stayed away, too. I wasn't honest with myself or you either."

God, I wanted her in my life so damn badly. "There's only one woman I want as mine for the rest of my fucking life, Eva." I moved my thumb so I could now brush it along her bottom lip. "There's only one woman I want as the mother of my children." I continued to brush that digit along the swell of her lip.

I was transfixed at what I was doing. And when she slipped just the tip of her tongue out and gently ran it along the pad of my thumb, I thought I'd come right then and there.

Christ.

"This is so crazy," she said, but it held no heat, no emotion.

"But it's also so right, Eva baby."

She didn't say anything, but she didn't have to. This was wild, untamed, and felt so fucking good. Damn, I hadn't even been inside of her yet, and I knew it would be the best I'd ever had.

"What if I don't want this ... whatever *this* is?"

I watched her mouth move as she spoke. "You don't want this? You don't want me?"

She shook her head but didn't say anything.

I grinned, but it wasn't one of amusement. "You can claim you don't want this." I leaned in close. "But you and I both know that'll be a fucking lie." I inhaled deeply, smelling the sweet scent that came from her. "I bet if I placed my hand between your legs you'd be wet for me, Eva." I leaned back an inch so she could get a good look at my face. "Are you wet for me, Eva?" I couldn't stop the low growl that left me at the thought she was primed for me, ready to take me into her body.

"Don't you think this is a little fast?" she asked softly and swallowed, obviously trying to seem reasonable. Hell, I was glad one of us could think straight. As it was, I was hard, possessive of her, and ready to take Eva right up against the fucking building.

"I've known you for years," I murmured and glanced at her mouth again.

Fuck, I want to kiss her.

"It was never like this, Dex."

"It should have been." I closed my eyes and groaned. "Say my name again." She was silent a second, and I looked at her again.

I felt her breath tease my face. "I like hearing it come from your mouth."

She didn't speak for long seconds, but that was okay. For her I'd wait for the rest of my fucking life.

"Dex, we should stop," she said, but there was no heat behind her words. She didn't mean them.

"If you truly want me to stop, then all you have to do is tell the truth, Eva. Don't fucking lie. If you don't want me, don't want this—"

"And what is *this*, Dex?" she said, cutting me off.

I lifted my hand and pushed the long fall of her hair away from her neck. "What I want is you, Eva. I want every part of you as mine. Only mine." I ran my finger along the side of her throat. Her pulse beat wildly beneath her ear, a testament to how worked up she was.

"And you just came to this realization?" she whispered.

I shook my head slowly. I pressed my rock hard cock

against her belly. "I just realized I was a fucking fool to try and ignore what I wanted."

"What you wanted..." She didn't phrase it like a question.

"You, Eva." I ground my erection against her. "You feel that?" I asked, but she didn't respond, just licked her lips. I could see the truth in her eyes. "Just tell me you want to be mine."

She parted her lips, but didn't speak. She was nervous, and I couldn't blame her for that. I was coming on pretty fucking strong, but it was like something had snapped in me. I couldn't wait, couldn't try and go slow and easy, even if she deserved that and so much more.

I leaned in close again so my mouth was by her ear now. "I want everyone to know you're mine."

She was breathing harder, faster, and I doubted she'd relax. Her hands were on my biceps, her nails digging into my flesh.

"When I say I want you as mine, I mean that and so much more, Eva." I slipped my hand along her side. Being a bold motherfucker, I placed my palm right between her legs. The skirt she wore gave way, and I growled low at the fact her panties were damp. "I want to own this sweet pussy, Eva."

She made the sweetest little mewling noise.

I nipped at her earlobe, and she dug her nails harder into my flesh. I added just a bit of pressure, but before I snapped at the pleasure I felt and took her right here, I moved my hand back up and placed my open palm right over her belly. My fingers spanned the width, and I leaned back to look in her eyes. "And every single time I take you, claim you as mine, Eva, I'll make sure to fill you up with my cum until you carry my baby."

She gasped.

"I don't want any other woman, don't want any other female to carry my baby." She didn't speak, but she sucked in a breath. "I want to fuck you with nothing between us. I want to be so far in you, so damn deep, that when I fill you up my seed comes out of you days later."

"Oh. God. Dex."

"I want my baby growing right here." I added a little pressure to her belly and watched her chest rise and fall rapidly. "Do you understand exactly what I'm saying?"

She licked her lips and nodded slowly.

"What do you think about that? How does that make you feel?"

She just shook her head, her whole body tight, her pupils still dilated, indicating how aroused she was.

"It scares me."

"But in a good way, doesn't it?"

She closed her eyes and exhaled. "God. Yes."

I grinned even though she couldn't see me.

Yeah, she was right here with me.

5

Eva

God, is this really happening?

Dex had his hand on my belly, and I couldn't deny what he said thrilled me, but it also scared the hell out of me.

He wanted me to have his baby.

He wanted me to be his woman.

Yeah, it scared me, and in a good way.

I'd wanted Dex for a long time, but I kept that hidden, moving on with my life. I wasn't going to pine over a man that never saw me as anything more than Charlie's little sister.

I pretended not to pine.

"Tell me you don't want this and I'll leave." His breath

brushed along my cheek. He smelled good, clean, manly. "It'll be hard as fuck, Eva, but I'll walk away."

The look in his eyes said he wouldn't give up that easily, and I knew that throughout the years when he'd wanted something he went for it.

Can I do this? Can I really give myself to Dex in all the ways he wants?

It was certainly what I'd wanted ... him, a family, and a life where I could actually be happy. I wasn't thinking about what Charlie might say, or thinking about what was right or wrong.

I was staring into Dex's eyes and seeing the desire, the need he had for me, reflected back, and all common sense and rational thoughts left me.

"I do want you."

He smirked, just a lift at the corner of his mouth. But damn, was it sexy.

He leaned in and claimed my mouth without saying anything in response. The way he stroked his tongue along mine sent this heat wave through my body. When he pulled away, I couldn't breathe. I was ready for him, so ready my panties were wet.

I would have agreed to anything right then and there.

But Dex stepped away when I thought he'd push this more. He smoothed a hand over my cheek, and leaned in once more to kiss me softly on my lips.

"Tomorrow I'm taking you out, Eva," he said quietly, his voice deep. "I'm going to treat you like a real woman, make you know how special you are." He ran the pad of his thumb along my bottom lip, his focus on my mouth still. "As much as I want you, and you better believe I fucking want you—" He reached down and ran a hand over the huge bulge pressing against his jeans. "—We need to start this off right, yeah?"

I nodded, not knowing what else to say.

"God, it's really fucking hard walking away right now, but I don't want to be a bastard. I don't want our first time to be me fucking you up against a wall ... even if that's what I want right now."

I knew he was hard, had felt it pressed against my belly. I wanted to tell him I didn't care as long as he was with me right now. But I bit my lip and stayed still.

"Until tomorrow, baby." He turned and left.

I could only stand there and watch him leave. Right before he got into his vehicle, he turned and looked at me. The way he winked had my pussy clenching painfully.

I wanted him, and I knew when I told him that it sealed my fate.

But was I ready to be the woman Dex wanted? Was I ready to give him what he wanted?

———

Eva

THE FOLLOWING EVENING

"You're going out with who?" Charlie asked, although he knew damn well.

I looked over at him. I was in the bathroom, getting ready for the dinner Dex had planned for us, and feeling all kinds of nervous.

"Dex," I said again. "I told you that on the phone, you know, right before you came over here."

Charlie had always been protective of me, even when we were younger, and I knew that's what he was doing now. It might be Dex, his best friend, but it was still a guy I was going out with. It being Dex just made it a little more complicated.

"Why?" Charlie asked and leaned against the doorway. He crossed his arms over his chest and just glared at me. I felt like my dad was interrogating me.

"Because he asked." I took a deep breath. "And I like him, Charlie."

My brother didn't say anything, and when I looked at him I saw this intense look on his face. "He's kind of old, yeah?"

I couldn't help it. I started laughing. "He's the same age as you." When Charlie doesn't say anything, I continued. "He's only ten years older than me." Charlie remained silent. I turned and faced my brother. "I mean, are you okay with me having dinner with him?" I wouldn't cancel my plans if Charlie wasn't because I was an adult, but I also didn't want this to be weird.

"Honestly?" he asked, not moving from his position and his focus intense.

"Yeah, of course."

He exhaled softly, his eyes trained on mine. "If there was one guy I'd want you to be with, it would be Dex."

Okay, that threw me for a little bit of a loop. "Really?" My eyebrows knitted, the tightness in my face letting him know my confusion was clear.

"I mean, he's no saint, but there's no one that'll look after you better than he will."

That made me feel all tingly, knowing Charlie approved of Dex and me, and even if he'd said a lot of intense things the other night, I didn't want to let this control me. I had to stay in reality; I knew if I let myself really go off the deep end, the fall would be devastating.

I looked down, my thoughts full of all the things that could go wrong. "I've cared about him for a long time." When I didn't get a response, I looked up at Charlie again.

"I know, Eva," he said softly. "I'm not blind. I've never been blind to the way you look at him ... and the way he's looked at you."

There I was, going through a loop again. "You did? He did?" I thought I'd kept how I felt to myself, but apparently not.

"You and Dex are both transparent as hell."

I felt my cheeks heat at this revelation, but it felt right, good even. "I thought this would bother you, even if it's only dinner."

Charlie shook his head. "It's not just dinner, not to him, Eva. I know Dex, and he doesn't do this kind of shit."

I didn't speak because I didn't know what to say.

"Hell, he hasn't been with a woman in a long damn time, and even before then he didn't sleep around. He always seemed distant in that regard."

Although I didn't want to really hear about Dex and anything he did with other women in the past, hearing that he hadn't been this major manwhore straight from Charlie felt really good.

It's not like I'd been celibate, but knowing Dex hadn't been with woman in a long time made me feel like things were going in the right direction. Maybe that was stupid of me, but if shit hit the fan, I'd deal with it then. Until that time—if that even happened—I was going to just roll with this.

6

Dex

We left the bar, but I wasn't damn near done with the night, and I hoped she wasn't either. I held the door open for her, and she stepped out of the restaurant. I wasn't about to deny myself and didn't give a fuck who saw ... I leaned in and inhaled the sweet scent that always clung to her.

I followed her out, and we walked in silence to the car. I was glad she'd let me pick her up. Eva could be headstrong, but if we were doing this, then I wanted to do it right.

"Let me get that," I said and unlocked the passenger side door for her. I held it open, watched her climb in, and saw a blush stealing over her cheeks. Truth was I

wanted to be a gentleman with her, but I also wanted her
so fucking badly. Doing something like holding the car
door open let me watch her long legs fold into the car as
she got in. It allowed me to see the slight rise of her skirt
as she shifted on the seat.

It allowed me to get my fill of her.

I must have stood there for too long, because she
looked up at me. "You got it engrained in your memory?"
she said, but I heard the teasing note in her voice.

I cleared my throat. I didn't get embarrassed very
often, but having Eva call me out on checking her out
had done just that. I closed the door and walked around
the car, my cock hard, but there was no way I was hiding
the fucker. I didn't want tonight to be about her thinking
all I wanted was a fuck.

I wanted her, of course. But this was about us
connecting on a deeper level. I hadn't lied or sugarcoated
what I wanted with her.

I wanted my baby in her.

I wanted her as my woman.

I wanted her as only mine.

But that didn't mean I wanted her to think all I
wanted was between her legs because she could see my
fucking hard-on.

I just needed to prove to her that I was right for her.

I needed to prove to Eva that I deserved her.

———

Eva

I LOOKED OVER AT DEX. He had one hand on the steering wheel, the other on the gearshift, and God, did it look sexy. The short-sleeved shirt he wore showed off his forearms, biceps, and tattoos. I'd always had a thing for muscular arms.

And he has arm porn going on for days.

I shifted slightly as my arousal rose. The entire time at dinner Dex watched me. He'd wanted me to talk about myself, to tell him things he didn't know.

He'd said he wanted to know everything about me.

And he'd been such an intense listener. I knew he heard every word I'd said, and although I'd never had anyone that interested in what I had to say, it felt good.

He was heading back to my house, and although he'd told me during dinner he was having a good time, he'd never pushed keeping the night going on longer.

But I wanted it to. God, I really wanted it to.

I didn't need to know every little detail about Dex to know what I wanted, and that was him, in every raw, hardened form he presented.

But even if we'd known each other for years, could I really be bold and tell him what I wanted, or how I really wanted this night to end?

I faced forward and swallowed.

"You know, even if you had told me to fuck off, I would have still tried, Eva."

I looked over at him, not really surprised. I knew Dex well enough that if he wanted something he went after it.

He didn't look at me, but I saw him smirk, and God, did it turn me on.

"Yeah, I know you well enough." I couldn't help but smile, too. We rode for another ten minutes before he pulled up in front of my house. I wasn't sure exactly what to say, but when I turned to face him, maybe to say good night, or hell, maybe to invite him in, Dex had his hand on the back of my neck and pulled me forward.

He kissed me hard, possessive, and as I rested one of my hands on his thighs, and the other on his shoulder to balance myself, all I felt was this intense need to be with him.

The feeling of his tongue moving in and out of my mouth, pressing against my tongue, had my pussy so wet I couldn't even breathe. But when he pulled me on top of him, I could feel the huge hardness of what was between his thighs. He wanted me; that was clear.

He pulled away just enough that we weren't kissing anymore, but our lips were still touching. "If I put my hand between your legs and touched your pussy, would you be wet for me, Eva?" he whispered against my mouth, and I breathed harder.

"I don't know, maybe you should find out." I was feeling pretty damn bold right now. I felt him smile against my mouth, but he didn't make a move to touch me. Instead, he took hold of my wrist in his hand and placed my palm flat on my chest.

"Show me, Eva."

I sucked in a lungful of air and slowly moved my hand down my body. He still had a hold on my wrist as I descended. Lower I went, our focus on each other. I stopped at my lower belly.

"Keep going, Eva." There was this fire behind his eyes, something that had me burning brighter, and I was about to get singed. But I didn't care.

I pushed my hand underneath my skirt, and as soon as I was under the material, he let go of my wrist and placed his fingers on my panties. I groaned, he closed his eyes, and together we blew out ragged breaths.

He rubbed me gently over my panties at first, but the longer he did that, and the more the seconds moved by, the faster he went. He was right over my clit, moving his finger back and forth over the swollen bud, and I knew I could come right then and there.

"Tell me what you want, Eva. Tell me and it's yours." His voice was so damn gruff. "Even if it's goodnight, I'll fucking take my hand away and kiss you goodnight."

"Is that what you want?" I pressed my lower body an inch down and rubbed my pussy back and forth over his hand, wanting to come desperately.

Dex didn't answer verbally. He just shook his head slowly.

"Tell me what *you* want," I whispered.

He didn't answer for long seconds, but he did keep rubbing me, making me suffer in the most incredible way.

"Dex—"

"The things I want to do to you are pretty fucking filthy, baby." He leaned in an inch and pressed his mouth firmly against mine again. He ran his tongue over my bottom lip and I shivered, feeling that pleasure build inside of me. "Do you want to come on top of me while we're parked in front of your house and I have my hand up your skirt?"

I wanted to say yes, that it really didn't matter where I was as long as he kept doing what he was doing. But, before I could say anything, he was speaking again.

"Or do you want to get off with my big dick shoved up your tight little pussy?"

Oh. God.

"You want to feel me filling you up with my cum, making you slick and hot from it?"

I moaned.

"You want me to make you feel so good you won't want anyone else but me?"

He stopped rubbing and pulled back. I forced my eyes open, looked at him, and tried to form a coherent thought.

We stared at each other for several seconds, both of our breathing jagged, the windows becoming steamy.

"You want my cock in you, don't you, baby?"

I nodded.

I wasn't even about to lie.

7

Eva

After I'd nodded, Dex hadn't wasted any time getting us into the house.

I kicked the front door shut with my foot, and Dex had me pressed up against the wall a second later.

"I want to be so deep in you, Eva," he groaned against my neck, and I turned my head and gave him better access.

He had his hands on either side of my head, caging me in, making me feel trapped, but in a good way.

"I want to pump you so full of my cum it comes out of you and makes your panties wet the next day."

"Dex. God," I breathed out.

"I want you so sore that when you sit down tomorrow all you can feel is me still inside you, Eva."

I didn't know if an orgasm could actually happen just from hearing someone talk dirty, but I'd find out soon enough.

He lowered his gaze to my mouth, his chest brushing along mine. "Being mine means you're my everything."

God, for such a strong, hardened man, Dex knew how exactly what to say to make me fall even harder.

I lowered my gaze to his mouth, my lips still tingling. "You sure you want to go there with me?" I whispered.

He lowered his head an inch closer to me. "Oh, yeah." He kissed me then, hard, possessively, demanding more. He started pressing his erection against my belly. He was huge, long, and so hard it was like he was sporting a steel pipe between his legs. "I want all of you, Eva," he murmured against my mouth.

I was more than willing to give all of myself to him.

He moved his hands down my face, stroked his fingers along the sides of my neck, and stopped right below my ears. Dex placed his thumbs at my pulse points, adding just the slightest pressure. It was so strange, but that small touch made everything in me come alive even more.

After a few seconds, he continued to descend my body. He stroked his tongue over my lips for only a second before delving into my mouth. When he was at my hips, he curled his fingers into my flesh and pulled me hard against him. I gasped, and his cock dug into my belly even harder.

He broke the kiss and started moving his mouth down my neck, stopping at my collarbone. When he ran his tongue over the bone, I shivered and dug my nails into his shoulders He hissed, but then groaned.

"That's it, baby. Give me more."

I breathed out heavily. I was so damn wet my panties were soaked clear through. A shiver worked its way through me when he went back to licking at my skin. It was like he was this wild animal.

My wild animal, and all this feral attention is for me.

"Touch me more, Eva."

I grabbed his head, tangled my fingers in his long hair, and pulled at the strands. He hissed out and lifted his head so we were eye level. A second passed with silence between us.

"Do it again," he gritted out.

I tugged at the strands hard enough his head went back and the tendons in his throat stood out in stark relief. But his eyes were locked on mine.

"You're so fucking hot," he said right before he slammed his mouth on mine. Our teeth clashed, our tongues fucked, and I was more than ready for whatever Dex wanted.

When he broke away this time, he flared his nostrils

for a second. I could see his mouth parted, his pupils dilated.

He's going to lose it, and it's all because of me.

I started breathing harder at that thought. It was like I was looking into the face of a feral animal that was about to snap.

I was the one to lean in and kiss him this time, and he groaned into my mouth. Dex grabbed my hair, and the force with which he pulled my hair had the pain mixing with pleasure.

After long seconds, he finally broke the kiss, and I wanted to beg him to fuck me already.

He rested his forehead against mine, our breath mingling. "I'm going to fuck you so hard, Eva."

He was rock hard, so big and thick. I was so aroused that wetness coated my inner thighs. Dex smoothed his hands over my ass, ran the pads of his index fingers along the crease where my butt and legs met, and then moved lower down the back of my thighs. He moved back up, and in the next second, he had my skirt and panties clean off of me.

I stood there, not sure what to do now, but Dex had plans, because he had my shirt pulled up and over my head. He tossed it to the ground and, in a matter of seconds, had my bra off, too.

Here I was, naked, aching, so damn wet, and ready for Dex to have his way with me.

My throat was so dry, but I managed to say, "Touch me."

He didn't make me wait. Dex placed his hand right between my thighs. His fingers were so big, slightly calloused, and I closed my eyes and exhaled roughly. He dipped his head and ran his tongue along my nipple, making the tip harder, more sensitive. He alternated between breasts for long minutes, all the while touching my pussy.

"Dex," I whispered and closed my eyes as his fingers found my swollen clit. He ran small circles around the bud then went back to rubbing his finger through my cleft.

He touched me for a few seconds, sucked and kissed at my skin until I was trembling, but before I could come, he stopped and stepped several feet back. I watched in rapt attention as he licked his fingers, sucking off my wetness.

"So fucking sweet," he growled. "You've always been mine, Eva." His head was downcast, but his eyes were locked on me. "I was just too much of a fucking idiot to accept it."

Power and strength radiated from him. I took in the wide expanse of his broad shoulders, followed the lines of his tattoos that wrapped around his arms and chest, and felt my heart jerk in my chest.

"You ready for me?"

I lowered my gaze, taking in that V of muscle that was

starkly defined. He might have his pants on, but his erection pushed at the fabric. It was huge, and I could only imagine what it would look like once it was freed.

I nodded.

I was more than ready.

8

Dex

There was nothing more I wanted in this world than the woman in front of me.

She's mine.

I felt like a fucking animal with her right now. Looking my fill of her naked body, my cock jerked at the sight. I wanted to fucking jerk off and just watch her, just see her smooth her hands over her body, those long fingers moving over the intimate parts of her. But I'd have plenty of time to take in every part of her ... memorize every single inch.

I saw her throat work as she swallowed. She was worked up, so fucking primed for me I knew if I touched her in just the right way she'd come for me.

I wanted her unhinged, but I also wanted to take my time, to make this last.

Yeah. Fuck. Right.

There was no way I was going to last tonight, not once I was deep in her pretty cunt.

"You're looking at me like you're starving," she whispered, her chest rising and falling as she breathed harder.

I growled low. Yeah, when it came to Eva, I was a fucking animal.

"I am, Eva." I moved an inch closer. "I'm so fucking hungry for you." I put my hand on her belly; her body trembled for me. "I want to put my baby in here. Right. Fucking. Here." She swallowed again, and I watched the line of her throat work through the act. "You want that, don't you?" I wanted to hear her say she wanted me to put my baby inside her. "Tell me how much you want to be mine. Tell me how much you want to be pregnant with my baby."

She closed her eyes and moaned.

"Look at me," I demanded and gripped her chin in my fingers.

She opened her eyes, her pupils fully dilated. "I want your baby in me. I want to be yours in every way."

Jesus.

It took all of my control not to fucking come right in my jeans.

Eva licked her lips, and I was riveted to the sight. The dirty images of her on her knees, with her mouth wrapped around my dick, slammed into my head. I was big, my cock thick and long, and she'd have a hard time working her mouth down all of it. But fuck, yeah, that would be hot.

I leaned forward and ran my tongue along the seam of her lips. I could easily become addicted to her.

I'm already fucking addicted to Eva.

"I am so damn hard for you."

She made this soft noise, one that sounded like need and desperation and everything that turned me on. I slipped my hand behind her nape, curled my finger into her soft flesh, and tilted her head to the side. I leaned down and ran my tongue along the side of her throat, feeling her pulse jack up higher.

"I'll make you feel so fucking good."

"You already are, Dex." She made another small noise and dug her nails into my skin. My cock jerked at the pleasure and pain.

I wanted this first time to be romantic, but I knew I couldn't go slowly with her. Hell, having her pressed up against the wall and dry humping the fuck out of her was hard as hell.

I dragged my hand up her belly and over her ribcage to cup one of her big breasts. I pushed my pelvis forward, grinding my jean-clad cock into her softness. I didn't move for long seconds, my thoughts becoming pretty damn real.

"I wish we'd gotten together years ago," I said softly,

meaning it down to my fucking marrow. I looked into her eyes, hoping she wasn't getting freaked the fuck out by what I said.

"Me too, Dex."

I closed my eyes; that thrill of pleasure had nothing to do with sexual gratification moving through me.

"We have now, though," she said.

"We have forever." I went back to sucking on her neck, dragging my tongue up the slender column of her throat, and I thrust my cock against her belly, back and forth, needing that friction, that closeness. Pulling back was hard as hell, but I managed to do it, because I needed to be inside her.

"As much as foreplay sounds pretty fucking incredible, I need to shove my nine inches into you, Eva."

I should have some kind of fucking control, or at least try and have it.

Here she was for me, naked, ready...

I had her in my arms a second later, strode to the bedroom, and kicked the door shut with my foot. When she was on the center of the bed, her legs slightly parted, her pussy a little hidden from me because it was dark in the room, I took a deep, steadying breath.

Control. I need to keep my fucking control.

"Take off your clothes," Eva whispered in this sultry voice.

I got the fuck out of my clothes, needing to be just as bare as she was. While looking at her body, taking in the long lines with shadows covering them, the rise of her large breasts, the dip and arch of her hips, I reached down and grabbed my cock. Her legs were long, smooth. Even her fucking feet were hot as shit.

I started stroking myself from root to tip, unable to control myself like some kind of teenager. But when I was around Eva, and especially now that she was giving herself to me, I didn't want to keep my control.

The tip of my dick was wet with pre-cum, and I ran my palm over the crest, my whole body tight.

"Show yourself to me, Eva." I didn't even try to mask the urgency or intensity in my voice. "I want to see what I'll be fucking owning tonight." And as she obeyed me instantly, all I could do was watch in rapt awe. "I meant what I said. Every. Fucking. Word."

I knew she was well aware of what I wanted with her. I'd made no secret of it. And if she had told me to stop, or she didn't want this, I would have backed the fuck off.

But instead of telling me that this was all too unreal, and that I'd lost my fucking mind, she breathed in and out slowly and said, "I know. It's what I want, too, Dex." She reached down, spread her pussy lips wide, and showed me exactly what was mine.

This was my woman, and together we'd make a baby, no matter how many times it took.

Hell, I was looking forward to it.

9

Eva

"Touch yourself for me," Dex said in this low, husky voice.

I parted my legs even wider, if that was possible, and touched myself, showed him the most intimate part of me. I wanted to make him feel good, wanted to please him. It wasn't a weakness, but a power.

I looked down at the long, thick length of his cock, and he was rock hard for me.

He was huge.

He stroked himself in slow motion. It was like he was always watching me, always keeping his attention laser-focused on me.

"You like watching me fucking jerk off? You like knowing what you do to me?"

I nodded, not finding my voice.

It was dark in the room, but I could clearly see the pre-cum coming out of the tip of his cock.

"This," he said and ran the tip of his finger over the crown of his cock, gathering that clear fluid, "will soon be in you."

My heart jumped into my throat. *I want that.*

"I'm going to pump so much cum into you the sheets will be wet because of it." He took a step closer. "But you want that, don't you?"

I nodded again and continued to run my finger up and down my slit, my body ready to take him.

He took a step closer until he was at the edge of the bed, his focus on my splayed thighs, watching me touch myself. I moved my finger to my clit and started rubbing the bud. A gasp left me as the pleasure slammed into me. Here we were, watching each other pleasure ourselves, and it was so damn erotic.

Dex stroked himself a little faster, the sound of his hand moving over his length, of flesh slapping against flesh, filling my head. His bicep contracted and relaxed from the rapid motion of jerking off.

"I could get off just watching you touch yourself, Eva." He groaned, took his hand off his dick, and finally moved onto the bed with me. He placed his hands beside my head and looked down the length of my body.

"I want this so badly," I said before I could stop myself.

"*I* want you so fucking badly," he said and looked at my face. He hovered above me, his huge body looming over me, making me feel so very feminine.

"After tonight, there's no going back."

I didn't want to.

"After tonight, you're finally mine." He leaned in close, but didn't kiss me. "Tonight, I finally claim you, Eva."

"I've always been yours," I said without realizing it, even if we'd gone our separate ways over the years. That didn't matter because we were here now, together. But the words were already out, and I could see they made Dex happy.

Kiss me.

Maybe he needed it as much as I did, or that I'd said it out loud, but Dex had his mouth on mine seconds later. I couldn't stop the small noise that left the back of my throat. And it was as if that sound made something in Dex snap, because he made this distorted sound, grabbed a chunk of my hair behind my head, and jerked my head back.

With my head back, my throat arched, bared, he started to kiss and suck the side of my neck again. He was thorough with his tongue and lips, making me squirm beneath him, ready to beg for his cock in me.

I felt the hot, hard length of him press between my thighs, right through my slit. He started moving his hips back and forth, rubbing himself through my clit.

I looked down as much as I could, and with the way Dex hovered over me, I could see his cock sliding through my cleft. It was so arousing, and I knew I could get off from this alone.

His cockhead moved against my clit every time he pressed his dick upward. I groaned at how good it felt.

"How much do you want me in you?" he whispered by my ear.

I wanted to feel him stretching me, pushing into me hard, demandingly. I wanted to feel like I'd split in two.

"You know how much I want it."

Dex didn't say anything else; he just started to swirl his tongue around the shell of my ear, causing my lips to part and my eyes to close.

Without breaking away, he reached between our bodies, grabbed his cock, and placed the tip at the entrance of my pussy. Everything inside of me stilled, tensed. He pulled back so our faces were an inch apart. For long seconds, he did nothing but stare into my eyes, his cock poised right there. If I just shifted, I could impale myself on him.

"I can't go slow, and there is no going back, Eva."

All I could do was nod. I didn't want slow, and I didn't want to go back. I just wanted us to move forward.

In one, deep, hard thrust, he shoved all those huge inches into me. My back arched, and my breasts were thrust out. He groaned above me, closed his eyes, and I saw, felt, how taut his body became. His balls were pressed right up against my body as he buried himself all the way in me. I was stretched to the max, the pain mixing with the pleasure, making me hungry for more.

When he started moving in and out, faster and harder with each passing second, I didn't stop myself from grabbing onto his biceps. Perspiration covered both of us in thick droplets. His massive chest rose and fell as he breathed, pumping in and out of me.

"Fuck," he said harshly. He pushed in and pulled out, over and over, groaning with every thrust and retreat.

I wanted to see what he was doing, so I lifted up on my elbows and looked down the length of my body. I saw his cock moving in and out of me, glossy from my juices.

I lifted my gaze to his abdomen, seeing his six-pack clench and relax with every thrust he made into me. "You like watching me fuck you?" he asked, sounding out of breath.

When I couldn't hold myself up anymore because he was making me feel so good, I fell backward. Once I hit the mattress, it was as if something shifted in Dex. He went primal on me then. His pelvis slapped against mine, the sound of sloppy sex so fucking arousing.

He pulled out, and I gasped in surprise and disappointment, but Dex flipped me over onto my belly, smoothed his hand along the side of my body, and made this low sound of need.

He didn't make me wait long to shove those nine

inches into me again. Dex palmed my ass with his big hands and gripped the mounds almost painfully.

God, that feels good.

"So fucking perfect." He grabbed my waist in a firm hold and hauled me up so I was now on my hands and knees. I felt so bare in this position, but it was the best kind of vulnerability. Dex pushed my legs wider apart with his knee; now my pussy was on full display, my lips parted for him.

He smoothed his hand over my left ass cheek, gently at first, but I wasn't fooled. Dex was raw in every way. He gave my ass a hard spank, and I jerked and gasped in pleasure.

"I'm not going to stop until you're pregnant with my baby, Eva." He ran his hand up my back, right over my spine. "And when my seed takes inside of you, you'll know what it means to be mine."

I'd never get sick of hearing him say how he wanted to get me full with his baby.

Never.

He speared his hand in my hair, yanked my head back, and growled. With his hand in my hair, he used his other one to reach between us and place himself back at my pussy hole. In a fluid motion, he shoved back into my pussy.

"*Jesus,* Eva."

"Oh. God. *Dex.*"

He moved in and out of me slowly, but after a few

seconds, he started picking up speed. Soon, his flesh was slapping against mine. He let go of my hair and gripped my hips with both hands, pulling me back on his cock as he surged forward.

He grunted, and my pleasure increased. Dex held my hips so tightly the pain had me gasping out. But it was the pleasure that overrode everything else.

"Fuck. Yeah." He thrust into me once, twice, and on the third stroke, he shoved deep and hard into me before stilling. "God, I'm going to come, baby." His nails dug into my skin, and I came, my pussy clamping down hard on his dick. He filled me up with so much of his seed, I swore I felt it as he came.

"Mine. You're mine forever, Eva." He jerked above me, still coming.

Then, after a few seconds, he covered my back with his chest, and his breath, coming out in hard pants, bathed my flesh in this humid, arousing sensation. Dex pulled out of me, and I couldn't stop myself from collapsing onto the mattress. I breathed hard against the sheets, trying to get my heart to still its rapid rhythm. Dex lay beside me, pulled me close, and placed his hand right between my thighs.

"I want my cum to stay in you, Eva. It belongs inside of you." He kissed the curve of my shoulder.

My skin was damp with perspiration, but it was nice because I knew exactly why I was sweaty. Dex pushed his finger into my pussy, and I shook and moaned.

"I want it inside of you," he murmured as he pushed his seed back into my body when it started slipping out of me.

"God, Eva," he said huskily.

This warm feeling filled me when he leaned down and kissed the top of my head.

I didn't know what the future held, no matter what either of us said, but I knew one thing... this felt pretty damn good.

Maybe this all should have felt more confusing, more insane. But to be honest, it felt like the most perfect thing in the world.

And I didn't want to let that go.

———

Eva

I LAY BESIDE DEX, listening to his deep, even breathing. It could have lulled me to sleep, but I was too deep in thought to get some rest.

I shifted, but he made this deep grunt, rolled over toward me, and wrapped his arm around my waist. He pulled me in close to his hard body, and I melted against him, loving that even in sleep, he wanted me close.

All of this felt so foreign in a sense, but it also felt right, like this was right where I was supposed to be. I lifted my hand and smoothed my fingers over the definition of his biceps. His muscles flexed beneath my touch, and he made this deep sound in his throat, one that sounded like he was thoroughly content and happy.

It's exactly how I feel right now.

I shifted once again so that my chest was pressed to his. He slowly opened his eyes, and if possible, he looked even sexier with that post-sex, hazy look of relaxation covering his face.

"Hey, you," he whispered, his voice so deep, so husky it speared right into me.

"Hey right back." I lifted my hand and cupped his scruff-covered cheek, smoothing my fingers along his face.

"This is real," he said without making it a question.

I stared right into his eyes.

"This is real," he said again and placed his hand on my belly. "Everything I said was the truth, Eva." He leaned in and kissed me, and I felt my heart flutter a bit. "I won't let you go. You're mine."

I'd jumped head first off a cliff, and although I didn't know what the future held, I was looking forward to reaching the bottom ... because I knew Dex would be there.

10

Eva

Five weeks later

I held the plastic bag in my hand, my fingers wrapped tightly around it, and my heart thundering.

Over the last month or so, Dex and I had been inseparable, or rather, Dex hadn't wanted me out of his sight. We spent our free time together, but it wasn't just having incredible sex—even though he was insatiable, and I was more than okay with that. He lavished attention on me, showed me a bad boy could have a softer, gentler side, too.

His protectiveness might not fly with some women, but for me, I was all about it. Heck, his jealousy over a guy even looking at me, the fact he wanted to stake a claim, even if that was glaring at said guy and wrapping his arm around me in ownership made me feel pretty damn wonderful.

"That you, baby?" Dex called out from somewhere in the house, and I took a deep breath. We weren't living together, but I spent a lot of time at his place, and when I wasn't here, he was at my house.

"Yeah," I called out. I didn't want to tell him what I was doing, especially if it came back negative. I don't know why I didn't just come out and tell Dex I was taking a pregnancy test. We never used protection, and we both knew what the result could be because of that.

He was hoping for a baby, and he made no secret of that.

And even though I'd never actually told him I wanted that too … I did.

I went into the bathroom, shut and locked the door, and pulled out the pregnancy test. Maybe I should have gotten more than one, but I didn't want to be a freak about this. I also didn't want to get his hopes up, or mine for that matter, by saying anything. I'd been late plenty of times in my life, and it had never been because I might have been pregnant.

I read the directions three times, although I was pretty sure this was all self-explanatory. I'd also seen enough movies with chicks peeing on the stick and waiting for the results that I knew the drill. But still, I read the damn pamphlet again and again.

When I pulled out the stick and eyed it, my heart started beating double time.

I did the whole unwrapping, taking the cap off, and before I did the whole peeing on it thing, I stared down at this little white and purple test.

After getting my thoughts as clear as I could, I finished it off, put the cap on, and set it on the counter. While I waited for it to do its thing, I washed and dried my hands and then stared at my reflection. My hair was piled up on my head, the heat making things unbearable. I lowered my gaze to my breasts. They were fuller, so sensitive even wearing a bra was a little uncomfortable.

After I figured enough time had passed, I reached out to take the stick off the counter. My hands shook, and my heart momentarily stopped. I looked down at the little clear window, my throat tightening even further at the results.

Pregnant.

I stared down at it for long seconds, making sure I was reading it correctly. On instinct, I placed a hand on my belly and looked at my reflection again. The woman who stared back at me had wide eyes and a look of shock on her face. It was after the initial surprise left me that I felt excitement.

I was pregnant.

I'm pregnant.

I turned around, unlocked the door, and pulled it open, and standing on the other side was Dex. He looked a little worried, maybe thinking something was wrong since I had hauled ass to the bathroom. But then he looked down at the test I held. A moment of silence passed, almost like time stood still, like this moment was frozen.

I lifted the test up so he could see the window, and although he could read it fine, I was sure, I still said, "I'm pregnant." Those words hung between us, and slowly he looked up from the stick to my face. "I'm pregnant, Dex." My voice was nothing but a whisper, and before I knew what was happening, he had me in his arms.

He had a hand on the back of my head, holding me to his chest. The warmth of his breath moved the hairs on the side of my face. He was tense, and now I was worried maybe something was wrong. Maybe he was having doubts? But before I could move or say anything, he pulled back an inch and looked down at me.

"You're pregnant," he said with a smile on his face, and I felt all the tension leave me.

"Is this crazy?" I asked, but I was smiling, feeling elation finally rise up, when just moment ago, it had been masked by my nervousness.

He cupped my face, stroked his thumbs along my cheeks, and the happiness I saw on his face made me love this man even more.

"You know how much I love you, Eva?" He kept

stroking my cheeks, and I knew he wanted me close. I could feel it in his touch. "I love you so fucking much." And surprising the hell out of me once again, Dex dropped to his knees in front of me and rested his forehead on my belly. "My woman. My baby." He pushed my shirt up and kissed the skin below my belly button. He looked up at me, the seriousness on his face evident. "Marry me," he said, and I was speechless.

"We don't have to get married just because I'm pregnant—"

He stood up, interrupting what I was saying. Taking my hand in his, Dex pulled me down the hall to his bedroom. He let go of me, walked over to the dresser, and when he opened it and pulled out a small black ring box, my heart jumped in my throat.

"I don't know when I planned on asking, Eva, but it's not because I wasn't sure." He turned around and showed me the ring. "I've had this for a couple of weeks, but was going to wait longer so it didn't look like I was crowding you." He moved closer to me, and I knew my body was shaking. "I also wanted to make this special, and for you to be sure what you wanted when I asked."

I breathed in sharply.

"I want you, not just as the mother of my baby, but as my wife." He pulled the ring out of the box and slipped it on my finger. "Marry me, Eva. You've already made me the happiest man in the fucking world, but I want *this* so damn badly, too."

I didn't want to cry, but God, I could feel it coming on. He placed his hand on my belly, smiling. "Yes," I whispered. He leaned in and kissed me.

"I think we'll be pretty kickass parents."

"Yeah, I think so, too."

––––––––

Dex

Four months later

THERE IT WAS ... *my* baby. I squeezed Eva's hand and looked at her. She was staring at the ultrasound monitor. She had this rounded belly, and I wanted to cover her skin, run my hand over the swell. My baby grew in there.

God, I love this woman so much.

"Do you want to know the sex?" the tech asked.

Eva looked at me then. "Do you?" I could hear the excitement in her voice.

I reached out and took her hand, giving it a squeeze, and nodded.

It took a few seconds while the tech was doing more measurements, more typing, but then she pointed to the screen. "Right there," she said and looked at us. "It looks like it's a boy."

My heart jackknifed in my chest, and I looked at Eva. She was smiling from ear to ear.

"We're having a boy," she whispered, and I couldn't stop myself from cupping her face and kissing her. I didn't give a shit if the tech was seeing this PDA. I'd always show my affection when it came to Eva.

The tech started cleaning off the gel from Eva's belly, and when that was done, I placed both hands on either side of her swelled stomach and leaned down to kiss her skin softly. Eva placed her hands in my hair, smoothing her fingers over my scalp.

I turned my face so I could see Eva. "I love you, baby."

She smiled in return. "I love you, too."

God, what I felt for Eva grew every single day.

It was the best fucking feeling in the world.

EPILOGUE ONE

Dex

Five years later

Life really had no meaning for me without the love of a woman and the laughter of my children filling my head.

And that's what I had.

I was the luckiest fucking man in the world.

I pulled Eva in closer to me, buried my face in her hair, and closed my eyes as I inhaled. She smelled incredible and felt so damn good in my arms. I slipped my arm around her and spanned my open palm on her belly. She was big and round with our fourth child. I was insatiable when it came to her and filling her with my cum; putting my babies inside of her only made me want her more.

I wanted her constantly, and seeing her healthy, glowing, and pregnant with what was mine, had proprietary need and possession claiming me.

She'd always be mine, no matter what.

Eva was due in about a month, and although she was probably sick of me wanting her like a fiend, she always let me have her. But then I made sure I had her coming twice before I got off.

I started rubbing her belly and felt my baby kick. I smiled. God, I loved this. She placed her hand on mine.

"I didn't wake you, did I, baby?"

She hummed softly and turned around to face me, although she made a little grunting noise in the process. "No."

Her sleepy smile had my cock getting hard once more. I knew she could feel it prodding her thigh, but she didn't give me a hard time about my voracious appetite when it came to her.

The years had gone by in a happy blur for me, and I did my best to make sure Eva and my kids were happy, safe, and cared for. I was the provider, and although Eva was more than welcome to work, she preferred staying home with the babies.

I rubbed her belly again, and my little girl kicked again.

"You think you can handle this baby girl, Dex?" She had her eyes closed, but a little smile covered her face.

With Jackson, our five-year-old, and Harlow and Mav,

our twin three-year-old boys, this baby girl coming into our lives was another blessing. But it also had every protective instinct coming out full force in me.

"If I can handle you, I can handle anything."

She opened her eyes and chuckled.

"But I do have some ground rules."

She lifted an eyebrow. "Oh yeah?"

"No dating for her until I'm dead." Eva chuckled a little harder. "And if a guy comes to the house asking her out, I'll show him my gun collection right before I break all of his bones."

She started laughing, the sound hitting me right in the chest. Seeing her carefree, even if she thought I was joking, had me feeling so fucking good.

"You don't even own any guns," she finally said, and wiped a tear from the corner of her eye.

"I'm buying stock in an arsenal as soon as she's born." I leaned in for a kiss. I slid my hand along her neck, cupped the side of it, and tilted her head back to really delve inside. She tasted sweet and fruity, and my cock jerked in response. We were both naked, and her big tits pressed against my chest.

"I'm sure the boys will be pretty protective of their baby sister, as well."

I grunted. "They better be."

I started kissing her again, and as the seconds passed, all I thought about was this moment.

"God, I could take you again right here, baby." But I

wouldn't because she had to be sore from the loving I'd given her just half an hour ago. I picked up her hand and kissed her ring finger. Her wedding ring scraped against my lips, and I kissed the rock again.

"If I could marry you all over again, I would, baby."

She smiled, her sleepy expression taking on a heated, more aroused look.

"Want to pretend it's our honeymoon again?"

I chuckled, and I was more than willing to give that a go. It might have been years since we'd gotten married, but for me, it felt like the first time every time with her.

This woman and my children were the reason I lived.

I looked down at Eva, seeing the love reflected back at me.

"What?" she whispered after I'd been staring at her for long moments.

"I love you so fucking much." I smoothed my fingers over her cheeks. "I'd die for you. Do you know that?"

She leaned forward an inch and kissed me softly. "I know."

Pushing down the blanket, I exposed her bared, rounded belly. I leaned down, ran my lips along her flesh, and framed her roundness. She ran her fingers over my hair, and I shivered at her touch.

My wife.

My life.

"Are you still happy?" I asked. I asked her this same

question often, not because I didn't think she was, but because I loved hearing her response.

"More than I could describe in words."

"You're mine," I said and looked up at her. I pulled her closer and just held her.

There was nothing more important than the woman in my arms, my baby in her belly, or the sons she'd given me.

"It's you." I stroked my fingers along her arm. "It's always been you." I leaned down to kiss the soft skin on her shoulder. "And it'll always be you."

The End

Now in audio!

More info can be found HERE

EPILOGUE TWO

HOLIDAY SONGS AND HOMEMADE APPLE PIE

Dex

Five years after the ending of Baby Fever

"She's so damn cute."

I smiled over at Eva. "Yeah, she is. She's doing so well, too, and she looks like a little badass up there on stage." I stared at my daughter, feeling so fucking proud. She might be five already, so not technically a baby anymore, but she'd always be daddy's little girl.

The boys were starting to get loud, and I glanced at them, giving them a "cut the shit now" look. They might be getting restless, but they'd respect their sister as she performed her first kindergarten holiday play.

"Oh, here she goes." Eva straightened, her hands up at her chest, and her smile wide.

And then my baby girl started singing. Of course it was a little nervous, and yeah, she might have forgotten some of the words, but shit, she was rocking it. I couldn't have been prouder.

There she was, this tiny little thing—taking after her momma—dressed as an angel, and singing her heart out. I had one of the boys' video tapping it all, because no way in hell was I about to miss having this as a permanent memory.

It wasn't long after that when the recital ended.

I made my way past the other parents, their "what the fuck" gazes latched on me. Yeah, I might not be the traditional father, not with my beard, manbun, and the tattoos covering my arms, but I was one hell of a dad. I knew that, strived for it.

I scooped Helena up in my arms and kissed her little head. "You made Daddy so proud, baby girl." She beamed up at me. I handed her over to Eva. Jackson, already ten, and our eight-year-old twins, Harlow and Mav, were acting like perfect gentlemen. I pulled Jackson in and ran my knuckles over his head, messing up his hair. He grinned and pushed me away.

"Stop, Dad."

I saw him glance in the other direction, and followed his gaze to where a little blonde girl his age was standing with her parents.

"Jackson has the hots for Bridgette O'Donnell," Harlow teased. That had Mav laughing and high-fiving his twin.

I should have told them to leave Jackson alone, but I could only shake my head and chuckle at the redness that covered Jackson's face.

"Harlow, Mav, your day will come soon enough," I said. I glanced at Eva, the woman I loved more than life itself. She pulled our four children closer to her, and listened to each of them go on about their childish rambling. All I could do was watch in wonder.

This woman was so fucking special to me. She was the mother of my children, my wife, and the one woman I'd lay my life down for in a heartbeat. I looked at my kids, each of them a little bit of us. I tried to be better each and every time for them.

It was always for them.

This was what I'd always wanted. My heart and life were filled with love and happiness, and fucking hell, could that make a man fall to his knees and thank the heavens for miracles.

———

Eva

I STAYED silent from the kitchen as I watched Dex read a Christmas story to the kids. The smell of the apple pie I just pulled out of the oven saturated the kitchen, the soft sound of holiday music coming from the radio, and the sight of the twinkling white lights and decorations scattered around the house made this calm settle over me.

Helena was already nearly asleep, curled up on Dex's lap. Seeing her rubbing a piece of Daddy's hair between her fingers as she dozed off had a smile curving my mouth.

Jackson and the twins were only half-ass listening, but they were being quiet, so there was at least that.

"Come on, bed time," Dex said, and I stayed back as I watched my husband, and the man I'd spend the rest of my life with, take our children to their rooms for the night.

I turned and grabbed a wine glass out of the cupboard, grabbed a bottle of wine off the rack, and went about popping the cork and pouring myself a glass.

I had just taken my first drink when I felt strong arms wrap around my middle. Dex pulled me back against him, and I stared down at his tattooed forearms and biceps. There wasn't anything on this man that didn't turn me on. All he had to do was look in my direction and I was so ready for him.

Like I was right now.

My panties were wet form my arousal, and my nipples were rock hard.

I also could feel his desire for me digging in the small of my back, that long, hard and thick pole he sported between his thighs making every feminine part of me rise up violently.

"You smell incredible," he whispered by my ear.

I closed my eyes and rested my head on his chest. "It's the pie." I felt him move his hand down my belly. He stopped at the junction of my legs, his fingers long, strong. A gasp left me when he added some pressure on my pussy with those manly digits. My jeans formed to the most intimate part of me.

"No, it's all you, baby. You smell so fucking good," he growled out low. "You always smell so damn good."

He spun me around and took the wine glass from my hand. I didn't stop this. No, God, I wanted this.

Before I knew what was happening, Dex had my shirt and bra off. The image of him sucking on my nipples slammed into me, and I was a second away from begging for him to do just that. But before I could utter a word, I watched as he grabbed a knife from the drawer, made a slice in the apple pie, and started to move his finger along the top where the apple pie insides were starting to come out. The smell of sweetness intensified, and my pussy grew wetter.

"Dex..." I whispered, but he didn't let me say anything else. Instead, he ran that apple pie filling-covered digit along my nipple. The flesh puckered up for him even more.

"You already taste so sweet," he murmured, and lowered his head to suck the tip into his mouth. The groan that came from him rocked me to my core. "But I couldn't resist doing this, baby," he said against my nipple. He took the next few seconds to suck the filling off my peak. He ran his tongue up and down, cupped my breasts, and made this animalistic sound.

"Baby, I need you."

"Then take me, right here, right now."

His groan was all I heard before he all but tore my pants off, lifted me off the ground, and set me on the kitchen counter. I watched as Dex unzipped and unbuttoned his jeans, pulled out his already hard dick, and stroked himself a few times. Even after all these years our sex life was still amazing, still like it had been in the very beginning.

It was passionate, raw, and all consuming.

"Hold on, baby, because I am so fucking primed for you." Dex stepped between my thighs and placed his cockhead right at my pussy hole. He stared into my eyes, and in one move buried himself fully in my body. I gasped at the intensity of his thrust, at being stretched, filled totally.

He fucked me then.

This wasn't about us making love, which we did plenty of times. This was about scratching that erotic itch we both had.

Dex pounded in and out of me, and soon sweat covered my body. My tits bounced between us, my breaths grew shallow, and I let myself go over the edge only minutes after he'd impaled me.

"Fuck, that's it. Come for me. Milk my cock. Take it all in."

I had my head tossed back, my eyes closed, and just rode out the pleasure. My pussy was contracting around his dick, and I could tell by the fast pumping coming from Dex, and the sounds that left him, that he'd fall over the edge very soon.

"Come on," I said, and forced myself to open my eyes and stare at him. "I want you to get off, too."

He grunted. "You want my seed all up in your cunt, baby?"

God, I loved his dirty talk.

I nodded.

"You want my jizz to slip from your tight little pussy when I pull out?"

I gasped, feeling another orgasm rising to the surface.

"Tell me," he demanded in a guttural groan.

"Yes, I want it all." And then I was getting off again.

"Yeah, that's so fucking it, Eva." He thrust once, twice, and on that third pump he buried his dick all the way in me. He came long and hard. I could see it on his face, on the way his entire body was so tense.

When he breathed out and stilled, I wrapped my arms around his neck and pulled him closer. He held me too, his head on my shoulder, the power coming from him tame after his orgasm.

"I love you," he whispered.

I stroked his back, and felt the cotton of his t-shirt damp from his sweat.

"I love you, too." He lifted his head and stared at me, and I cupped his beard-covered cheek.

"You're it for me."

I felt my heart jump at his words.

"You've always been it for me."

"I love you," I said again, and leaned in to kiss him. I tasted the subtle hint of apple pie on his tongue.

He pulled out with a groan, but had me cradled in his arms only seconds later, and was striding out of the kitchen.

"What are you going?" I asked, smiling.

"I'm going to run you a bath, properly wash that luscious body of yours, dry you off, and take you to bed." He stepped into our room and went into the master bathroom. "And when that's all said and done, I'm going spread your thighs, and eat your pussy out until you get off again. I'm going to make you come for me so many times you're exhausted from it." He set me on the edge of the tub and just stared at me for long seconds.

He cupped my cheeks, and the seriousness in his face went deep. "You'll love me forever?"

To hear this big, strong man asking me something so vulnerable could have had me crying. Even after all these years my love for him was stronger than ever.

"Because for me, it's just you, Eva."

I kissed him, and pulled back to look into his face this time. "Every day I love you more. That'll be how it always is, Dex."

He pulled me in close and just held me. This was nothing better than having this man hold me like I was his world.

"You are my world," he said, and I smiled.

Fairytale endings do happen. I was living proof of that.

ABOUT THE AUTHOR

Find Jenika at:

Instagram: Instagram.com/JenikaSnow
Goodreads: http://bit.ly/2FfW7A1
Amazon: http://amzn.to/2E9g3VV
Bookbub: http://bit.ly/2rAfVMm
Newsletter: http://bit.ly/2dkihXD

www.JenikaSnow.com
Jenika_Snow@yahoo.com